W9-AZM-441

WELCOME TO
PASSPORT TO READING

A beginning reader's ticket to a brand-new world!

Every book in this program is designed to build read-along and read-alone skills, level by level, through engaging and enriching stories. As the reader turns each page, he or she will become more confident with new vocabulary, sight words, and comprehension.

These PASSPORT TO READING levels will help you choose the perfect book for every reader.

READING TOGETHER
Read short words in simple sentence structures together to begin a reader's journey.

READING OUT LOUD
Encourage developing readers to sound out words in more complex stories with simple vocabulary.

READING INDEPENDENTLY
Newly independent readers gain confidence reading more complex sentences with higher word counts.

READY TO READ MORE
Readers prepare for chapter books with fewer illustrations and longer paragraphs.

This book features sight words from the educator-supported Dolch Sight Words List. This encourages the reader to recognize commonly used vocabulary words, increasing reading speed and fluency.

For more information, please visit www.passporttoreadingbooks.com, where each reader can add stamps to a personalized passport while traveling through story after story!

Enjoy the journey!

To Jennifer, Steven, and Philip

Little, Brown and Company

Hachette Book Group
237 Park Avenue, New York, NY 10017
Visit our website at www.lb-kids.com

Little, Brown and Company is a division of Hachette Book Group, Inc.
The Little, Brown name and logo are trademarks of Hachette Book Group, Inc.

The publisher is not responsible for websites (or their content) that are not owned by the publisher.

Abridged Edition: April 2013
First published in hardcover in April 1988 by Little, Brown and Company

LCCN: 2012029481

ISBN 978-0-316-21848-1

10 9 8 7 6 5 4 3 2 1

CW

Printed in the United States of America

Passport to Reading titles are leveled by independent reviewers applying the standards developed by Irene Fountas and Gay Su Pinnell in *Matching Books to Readers: Using Leveled Books in Guided Reading*, Heinemann, 1999.

The Dog
That Pitched
a No-Hitter

by **MATT CHRISTOPHER**
illustrated by **STEVE BJÖRKMAN**

LITTLE, BROWN AND COMPANY
New York   Boston

4

CHAPTER

The day was hot and muggy, the field was soggy from last night's rain, and Mike did not feel well. What pitcher would, Mike thought, if his team were trailing by nine runs?

The Lake Avenue Bearcats were beating the Grand Avenue Giants by a score of 19 to 10.

Why do we even have to finish this lousy
game? Mike wondered.

"Because it is the rules, pal," he heard
a voice in his head say. "And you know not to
bend the rules, right?"

Mike glanced over to the Giants' bench
and saw Harry, his dog, relaxing in the shade.

"Right," Mike answered him in his mind.

Mike and Harry shared a very special secret: They can communicate with each other through ESP, or extrasensory perception.

Mike had first seen Harry in an animal shelter and was surprised to discover that he could understand the dog's thoughts, and the dog could understand his! It was the start of one of the best friendships ever.

"This batter is easy," Harry was telling him now in his head. "Keep the pitches down by his knees."

Harry liked to watch the other team practice before the games so he could learn the players' strengths and weaknesses.

"If I had good control, I would try it," Mike said.

He stretched and threw a pitch.

The baseball streaked toward the plate—waist-high.

POW! The batter socked it high and deep to center field.

"No sweat," Mike heard Harry say.

"Frankie will catch it in his back pocket."

Frankie Tuttle, the center fielder, might

have been able to catch it in his back pocket if he

had tried, but he used his baseball glove instead.

Mike breathed a sigh of relief. One out.

Five more to go—two this inning, three the next.

The Bearcats' next batter came to the

plate. It was Bugsy O'Toole.

"He already has a homer and a triple," said
Mike. "Shall I walk him?"

"Keep them low and inside," Harry advised.

Mike aimed his pitch at the low inside
corner of the plate and managed to throw the
ball exactly where he wanted it to go.

Bugsy O'Toole swung at it and drove a
hot grounder to third base, but Jerry Moon
threw him out.

"There you go," said Harry.

Mike smiled. "Thanks, pal," he said.

CHAPTER

Mike was relieved for a while, but then the Giants could not get a man on base during their turn at bat. By the top of the seventh, the score was Bearcats 20, Giants 10.

The Giants failed to score when they batted for the last time, and the game went to the Bearcats.

"I should not have let that run score," Mike said with frustration as he and Harry headed home.

"You tried your best," Harry said.

Mike shrugged. "I hope the coach does not have me start against those Peach Street Mudders on Friday. They are tough to beat!"

"I know," said Harry. "They are numero uno."

Mike looked at him. "Numero what?"

Harry grinned. You could always tell he was grinning by the way his mouth curved up at the corners.

"Uno means one in Spanish," he said. "I have been learning a lot by watching television. Like this, for instance."

Harry stopped and did something Mike had never seen him do before. He did a crazy dance on his hind legs.

"What is that?" Mike asked, wide-eyed and laughing.

"You like it?" said Harry. "It is a dance called the Bunny Hop."

"You crazy dog! You better stop that before someone drags you off to the circus!"

"Yeah, right." Harry stopped his crazy dance. "From what I have heard about circuses, they are not for an intelligent creature like me."

Mike shook his head. "Harry," he said, "I do not know what to do with you. But I do not know what I would do without you, either!"

Harry hopped up into Mike's arms and licked his face.

CHAPTER

The next four days were difficult for Mike. He worried more about pitching against the Peach Street Mudders than he did about any homework or test his teachers could give him.

The Mudders had played four games so

far and won them all. Most of the players were

big guys who could hit a ball a mile long.

They were players like Barry McGee,

who averaged a home run every game,

and Turtleneck Jones, who was almost

as big and tough as Barry.

"I do not want to think about them,"
Mike said to himself while playing catch
with his father in the backyard. "Maybe I
will be lucky. Maybe Coach Wilson will have
somebody else pitch."

"You are worrying too much," said Harry,
who was resting comfortably under the shade
of a nearby tree. "All you need is control. I will
tell you what to pitch to each guy as he comes
to the plate, and you take it from there."

"Except I do not have control over my pitches,"
Mike grumbled. "All I have is speed."

"Did you say something, son?" his father asked.

Mike shook his head. "Sorry, Dad," he said.
"I was talking to myself."

Mike and Harry had made a pact that
nobody—not even Mike's parents—would find
out their secret, but sometimes Mike forgot to
communicate mentally with Harry and started
talking out loud.

At last came the day of the game against the Peach Street Mudders. And, as Mike had feared, Coach Wilson had him pitch.

The Mudders were first at bat, and Mike was scared from the start. He walked the first

batter and hit the second batter in the foot,

putting him on base, too. Then dark-haired

Barry McGee strode up to the plate.

"Pitch high and outside to him," said
Harry, who by now was lying by the stands.
"That is his weak spot. I watched him during
batting practice."

"I will try," said Mike.

But he was too nervous to follow Harry's
instructions. He stretched, and pitched.
The ball went straight over the heart of the
plate. Barry knocked it to center field, where
Sparrow Fisher caught it...then dropped it!

"Oh no!" Mike groaned as he watched two
runs score and Barry go safely to second base.

"Have faith, pal," Harry said. "Have faith."

"That is easy for you to say," Mike said.

Nobody else scored that inning or the next.
In the third, the Giants got three men on—one
on a walk, one on a passed ball by the pitcher,
and one on an error, a sizzling grounder through
the third baseman's legs.

The score was Grand Avenue Giants,
4, Peach Street Mudders, 2, at the top of the
seventh inning. Mike, nervous as a mouse
trapped in a room full of cats, hit the first
batter on the shoulder, walked the second,
and fumbled the third man's bunt.

"Oh no!" Mike groaned again. "No outs, and three men on base! What will I do now, Harry?"

A hit could tie the score. A long one could put the Mudders ahead. Mike's heart pounded.

"Harry?"

No answer.

Mike looked over to the stands, where he had last seen Harry. But there was no Harry.

Sweat glistened on Mike's face. "Harry!" his mind screamed. "I need your help!"

CHAPTER

"**P**lay ball!" cried the ump.

Just then the fans began to laugh.

Mike was flustered. What was so funny?

As the ball left his hand, he knew it was headed right toward the middle of the plate. He braced himself for the hit that was sure to come.

"Strike!" yelled the ump, to Mike's surprise.

The batter must have been distracted, too.

Mike sped another across the plate. "Strike two!"

And another. "Strike three!"

The fans kept roaring with laughter as the next batter—who was trying hard not to laugh, too—stepped up to the plate.

They must be laughing at me, Mike thought.

He struck out the second batter, too.

And the fans kept laughing.

Let them laugh, Mike thought to
himself. For the first time since the game had
started, Mike began to relax.

Then the next batter walked up to the plate.

It was Turtleneck Jones. He was not laughing.

He looked angry and determined.

But Turtleneck tried too hard.

"Strike one!" the ump called as Turtleneck swung at Mike's first pitch and missed it by a mile.

"Strike two!" the ump said as Turtleneck chopped the air a second time.

Then, "Strike three!" the ump yelled as Turtleneck swished for the third time.

CHAPTER

"**Y**ou did it! You did it!" Monk cried,

running to Mike from first base. "You

pitched a no-hitter!"

Mike's eyebrows arched. "I did what?"

He suddenly realized the game was over.

"Nice game, Mike," said Coach Wilson

as he patted Mike on the back. "But I think

you got a little help from that dog of yours."

Mike stared at the outfield, where Coach Wilson was pointing. There, doing a crazy, twisting dance on the platform in front of the scoreboard, was Harry.

"Oh no!" Mike cried. "Is that what the crowd was laughing at?"

"The crowd, and some of the batters, too," said the coach. "I think you owe that dog a few extra dog biscuits tonight, Mike."

Mike grinned. "I sure do!"

Seconds later, Harry came sprinting across the baseball field toward him.

"Harry!" Mike cried as the dog sprang into his arms. "What the heck were you doing?"

"The Bunny Hop, remember?" said Harry. "Want to see me do it again?"

He jumped to the ground and started kicking out his legs.

Mike laughed and then stopped to look at Harry.

"Why did you leave me alone out there, anyway?" Mike asked.

"I never left you," said Harry. "I just took some of the pressure off by entertaining the crowd a little."

"Is that cheating?"

Harry turned serious. "No way! You did it by yourself all along. I saw you stand up to Turtleneck Jones."

Mike remembered how relaxed and in control he had felt. "I guess you are right," he admitted.

"Of course I am right," Harry said. "All you needed was some confidence."

"And a dog who dances like a rabbit!" Mike said, grinning.

"Naturally," said Harry, who Bunny Hopped all the way home.